W9-BSQ-529

Jag

Story developed with Dean Sheremet

Special thanks to Jan Miles

Text copyright © 2003 by LeAnn Rimes Entertainment

Illustrations copyright © 2003 by Byron Preiss Visual Publications, Inc.

All rights reserved.

CIP Data is available.

Published in the United States by Dutton Children's Books,

a division of Penguin Young Readers Group

345 Hudson Street, New York, New York 10014

www.penguin.com

Printed in USA

10 9 8 7 6 5 4 3 2 1

First Edition

ISBN 0-525-47155-3

LeAnn Rimes

Jag

ILLUSTRATED BY RICHARD BERNAL

A Byron Preiss Book

DUTTON CHILDREN'S BOOKS • NEW YORK

In a dense, cool corner of the rainforest, the great hunter waited under a large leaf. Silently, one paw slid forward. Then another. The hunter crept along, belly on the ground, until almost upon the target. Finally, she leapt with a snarl and . . .

. . . the butterfly she was hunting yawned, shook its tiny head, and fluttered on to the next vanilla blossom.

The hunter paused and took a deep breath, just as her mother had taught her. She then let out a terrific roar for a tiny jaguar.

Not only did the butterfly tumble from its flower and take flight, but a hundred other colorful butterflies swarmed into the air, much to her delight.

Day after lazy day, Jag—an only cub—
played in the forest. She frolicked in sunbeams,
hopped along with friendly frogs, and lay on
her back watching bright birds soar.

She also loved to climb the monkey ladder
to her favorite tree branch. At the top of the
tree lived Isabel the parrot, a much older
creature who today, as always, appreciated
young Jag's visit.

"Well, hello, Jag," Isabel said. "I suppose
I'll be seeing less of you soon, eh?"

Jag was starting school in a few days
and scowled at the thought of it.

"What's the matter?" Isabel asked.
"Aren't you excited? Fishing and climbing
and roaring and swimming lessons . . . "

"You know I hate swimming. Mom is
making me try it again today," Jag said
unhappily. Nothing frightened Jag more than
the river. She preferred solid ground, which
didn't shift and slip under her paws.

"You'll learn to love it, just like you'll love getting to know other jaguars your age."

"Who needs that stuff?" Jag said, wrinkling her nose.

Isabel, who was very wise, said, "*You* do."

Along the way to the river, the bright birds were soaring, the butterflies were swarming, and the friendly frogs were hopping. But Jag had to walk past them all. The next thing she knew, the *swoosh* of rushing water was in her ears.

"Come along, Jag," her mother sang. "What a perfect day for swimming!" And with that she splashed into the water and paddled into the middle of the river, where she floated, belly up.

Jag poked a toe into the river and shuddered, thinking about how deep the water was. Then she thought about how sturdy the ground was.

She glanced over at her mother, who was gliding with the current. Then, with a sigh, Jag turned around and took off. When her mother looked over, all she saw was the tip of Jag's tail disappearing into the forest.

Jag ran straight to her tree and quickly climbed up to her branch. She lost her footing only once.

"See, I'm a good climber," she said out loud.

"So you are," observed Isabel from above.

Jag plopped down on her branch, miffed. "And I can roar, too!"

"So you can," Isabel chipped in.

"So who cares about stupid old swimming," Jag said.

"Ah," Isabel said. "So that's what this is about. You know, if you don't face up to this fear, it will grow into a bigger problem. The others in school might think it's silly that you're afraid of the water."

Jag pouted. "No, they won't!"

Isabel cocked her head to one side.
"Well, the way I see it, you're going to have
to stand up to something very soon. Either
your fears or your peers. And the way
you're going, probably both."

Frowning, Jag mumbled, "You're
wrong. You'll see."

On the first day of school, Jag's mother dropped her off with a forehead nuzzle and an "It'll be fine."

"But suppose Isabel was right? Suppose they laugh at me?" Jag winced at the thought.

"You'll do great," her mother said, "and I'll be back to pick you up in no time."

Jag nervously took a seat with the class.

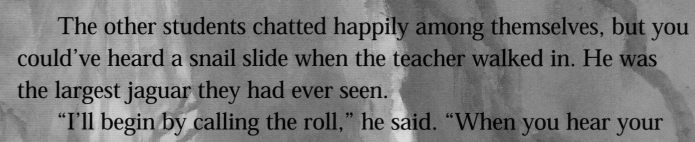

The other students chatted happily among themselves, but you could've heard a snail slide when the teacher walked in. He was the largest jaguar they had ever seen.

"I'll begin by calling the roll," he said. "When you hear your name, stand up and say 'Present.'"

"Anna!"

PRESENT!

"Danny!"

"Present!"

"Hank!"

"Present!"

"Jacqueline!"

There was silence. Jag stood and said, "Please . . . call me Jag." The silence lasted only one second after she finished speaking, then the snickering started.

"**What kind of name is Jag?**" someone jeered.

"Who's next? Ow the Owl?" cried someone else.

The class hooted with laughter! The more they giggled, the hotter Jag's face got.

By the end of the day, Jag had learned that most of the jaguars in her class were related to one another. "It's not fair," she complained when she got home.

"They already knew each other," she grumbled over dinner.

"They laughed at me," she moaned as she went to bed.

"It'll get better," her mother said as she tucked her in.

That night Jag couldn't sleep, so she counted her spots. She counted one side, then rolled over and counted the other. After that, she closed her eyes and did it from memory.

But nothing worked. She tossed and turned until the sun came up.

The next day wasn't better. The teacher declared that they would begin swimming lessons that morning. Jag was terrified. The teacher took them out to a quiet part of the river and lined them up alphabetically.

"We'll begin by having you hold your face in the water for ten seconds." He called on Anna. Then Danny. Then Hank.

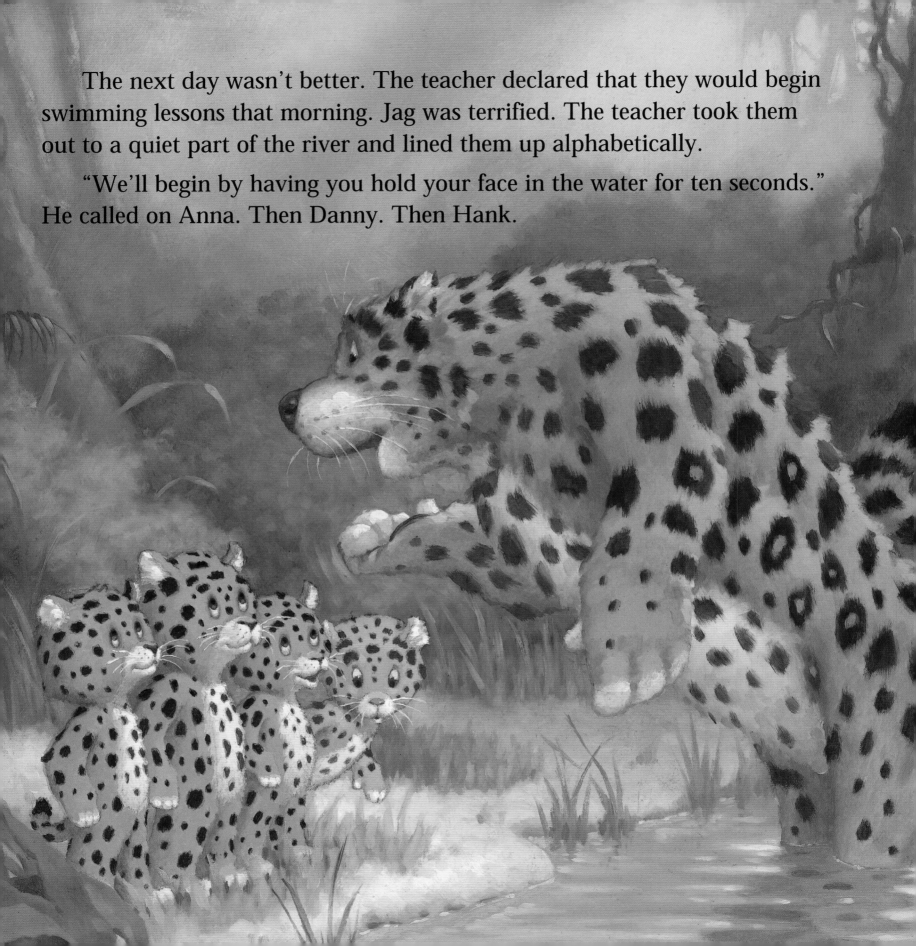

Then he called on Jag. Her fur stood on end and her legs shook. She crept to the water and lowered her face.

As she got closer, a small fish jumped up and startled her.

Jag yelped and tried to back away quickly, but the wet grass under her paws made her fall. Boy, did the class laugh at that!

"Quiet, class!" the teacher growled. "What seems to be the problem?" he asked Jag. Anna, Danny, and Hank poked each other and giggled, their fur still dripping. Jag didn't answer.

"Well, go on," the teacher said. He pointed at the water. But instead of moving forward, Jag trembled and started to retreat. Everyone was watching her, and she wished she could disappear.

"She's afraid of fish!" Anna whispered loudly.

Jag spun around and cried, "Am not! I'm not afraid of fish!"

"Then what's the problem?" said the teacher impatiently. "In you go!"

"I can't!" she cried. "I just can't!"

"Why not?" the teacher bellowed.

"Because . . . " Jag whimpered, "I'm afraid . . . of . . . of . . ."

Jag was still stammering when Danny pointed in her direction and said, "Holy howler monkeys!" The entire class began to point and laugh.

Jag turned on her heels and tried to make a dash for the forest, but something was right in her path. She bumped into it and fell again.

The something turned out to be what the
class was pointing at—a small jaguar with
completely black fur. "Have you ever seen a
jaguar with no spots?" Hank called out.

The black jaguar reached to help her
up. "Hi, I'm Simon," he said. "I'm new."

Hank pulled Jag toward their group. "Careful! It might be contagious!" he cried.

Jag smiled nervously, grateful not to be the butt of the joke this time. The others clung to her, tears of laughter running from their beady little eyes. The teacher called for order.

Simon dropped his head and started to walk off. Jag knew exactly how he felt. She hesitated a moment, then pulled away from the other jaguars.

She ran over to Simon and put a paw on his shoulder.

"Wait," she said, "don't go."

"Why not?" he replied.

"Because . . ." Jag repeated Isabel's words, "you have to stand up to your fears. And sometimes your peers."

With that, she took a *deeeeeep* breath and turned back to face the laughing jaguars. She released a roar that shook the vines, rippled the water, and made nearby monkeys gasp and clutch their tails. When she finished roaring, there was silence. And no small amount of trembling.

"Wow," Simon said.

Jag smiled. "My name is Jacqueline," she said, "but I think the nickname Jag is cooler, don't you?"

"Yeah, you're definitely more of a Jag," he nodded.

"Wanna play after school?"

He grinned a toothy grin. "You bet."

The great hunters waited under large leaves and leapt playfully at their targets. They frolicked, hopped, and climbed until the insect musicians of the forest signaled the coming of night. Before heading home, Jag stopped by to introduce Simon to Isabel.

"A friend, eh?" Isabel asked,
looking down at Simon.
Jag beamed.
"Who needs that stuff?" Isabel
squawked.
"*I* do!" said Jag. "Much more
than swimming lessons!"